MISSISSIPPI
BRIDGE

MISSISSIPPI BRIDGE

Mildred D. Taylor

PICTURES BY

MAX GINSBURG

DIAL BOOKS FOR YOUNG READERS • *New York*

Published by Dial Books for Young Readers
A Division of Penguin Books USA Inc.
375 Hudson Street • New York, New York 10014

Text copyright © 1990 by Mildred D. Taylor
Pictures copyright © 1990 by Max Ginsburg
All rights reserved • Printed in the U.S.A.
Designed by Amelia Lau Carling

W
5 7 9 10 8 6 4

Library of Congress Cataloging in Publication Data
Taylor, Mildred D.
Mississippi bridge / by Mildred Taylor; pictures by Max Ginsburg.
p. cm.
Summary: During a heavy rainstorm in 1930s rural Mississippi,
a ten-year-old white boy sees a bus driver order all the black passengers off a
crowded bus to make room for late-arriving white passengers and then set off
across the raging Rosa Lee Creek.
ISBN 0-8037-0426-7. — ISBN 0-8037-0427-5 (lib. bdg.)
[1. Race relations—Fiction.   2. Afro-Americans—Fiction.
3. Prejudices—Fiction.   4. Southern States—Race relations—Fiction.]   I.
Ginsburg, Max, ill.   II. Title.
PZ7.T21723Mi   1990   [Fic]—dc20   89-27898   CIP   AC

In memory of my beloved father, the storyteller.
Once again I have drawn from one of the stories he told.

M. D. T.

It was raining and had been all the day. Fact, it had been raining for some weeks, a steady, big drop kind of rain that had roads all slopped up outside and ceilings all swollen up and leaking inside. Our ole Mississippi winter it was almost finished, but not quite. In those there last few days before spring, folks had to go looking for things to do. Mostly, the womenfolks, they found something; womenfolks could always find work. Ma and my sister, Lillian Jean, they stayed inside and cooked and sewed and ironed and quilted and cleaned. But there was nothing much for menfolks to do but wait out the rain, wait for the dry-out and wait to plow and wait to plant. Pa and my brothers, R.W. and Melvin, and me, we had done chopped up all the wood needed chopping, mended all the fences and tools needed mending, and bought our seed, so we just waited.

Pa passed a goodly amount of his time up at the Wallace store. R.W. and Melvin, who were near to man-size theyselves, spent considerable hours up there too. Pa and R.W. and Melvin and the other men who gathered there would sit around that old potbellied stove. They'd play checkers some, but mostly they just talked about the hard times. They laughed and told stories and done some joking and Ma said that all helped them to pass the time, helped to ease the worry about cotton prices. Cotton had been down lower than ever for a long spell—more than two years—ever since the Depression come in '29 and everything hit bottom. It ain't looked like prices were ever going to rise up again and Pa said if they didn't get to rising soon, we would all be living worse than Negroes.

There were a many days I gone up to the Wallace store

myself. I ain't had much age on me then. I was only ten so I ain't sat much with the men inside. 'Stead, I'd sit myself right there on the floor boards of the porch, lean against a post, and watch the crossroads. Course now, watching the roads ain't meant there was that much to see, just the forest all around and the slop of red mud. Every now and again a truck would come along or a wagon or somebody'd come walking up the road heading for the store. About once the week the bus come down this way from Jackson, made a stop in front of the store to pick up folks, then gone on west over the bridge that crossed the creek called the Rosa Lee. The next day, it come back up again, heading north. Most days, though, I just sat on that porch, looking out at the rain and the gloom and ain't nothing much happened to break the expectedness of it all.

Fact to business I was sitting there the day Rudine Johnson and her mama come up the road carrying a couple of string-tied suitcases and looking like they were about to travel. There was a low fog and I seen them step out of it on a sudden, almost like haints in the night. Rudine was of good age, near to the same as R.W. and Melvin, and I ain't know'd neither her nor her mama too well, so all I done was give a nod and they done give a nod back, then they stepped past me and gone in the store.

I ain't paid them no more attention after that, leastways not till I heard Mr. John Wallace laugh. Then I turned round and looked inside. Rudine, she was standing front of the counter and her mama was right side of her. Rudine, she was kind of fingering a wide brim, summer-sky-blue hat with the tiniest little sprig of spring-like flowers tucked off to one side of it. The hat was sitting on a counter stand and Rudine, she was asking of Mr. John Wallace, who owned that store, if maybe she couldn't try it on. That was how come Mr. John Wallace was laughing.

"Now, Rudine, you know I can't let you try on that hat," said Mr. John. "You can buy it now, but once you do, you gotta keep it. Can't be bringing it back for no exchange, not after you done put it on your head."

"Yes, suh . . . I knows . . ." She looked kind of longing like at that hat, then she done sighed deep and shook her head. "Well, I don't 'spect it matter none. Can't buy it noways."

"That's what I figured," said Mr. John Wallace, then he turned back to Pa and R.W. and Melvin and the other men sitting around the stove. "Niggers," he snorted, then he done laughed again.

Just 'bout when he done that, Miz Hattie McElroy and her granddaughter, Grace-Anne, come riding up. Miz Hattie was a widow lady. She used to be my teacher and she lived right up the road from the Jefferson Davis School. Uncle Moses Thompson, an old colored man, who done a lot of odd-job work for Miz Hattie, was driving. He stopped the car 'right side of the gas pump, got out, and opened the door for Miz Hattie and Grace-Anne. Grace-Anne was a pretty girl, not more than maybe four years old. She had sunshine curls and eyes green as new pine tree needles. I liked her and I liked Miz Hattie too. They was quality folks.

" 'Ey, Jeremy!" squeaked Grace-Anne in that tinkle of a little voice.

" 'Ey," I done returned.

"Jeremy, child!" spoke Miz Hattie. "What you doing here all alone? Your daddy inside?"

"Yes, ma'am," I said. "Him and R.W. and Melvin."

Miz Hattie seemed a mite displeased 'cause she give a frown. "Well, they most times are, aren't they?" she said, and I wasn't sure how to take that. I wasn't sure if that was a slur against my daddy. Then she turned back to Uncle Moses Thompson. She spoke to him a few minutes, words out of my hearing, and then Uncle Moses took out the bags, set them on the porch, and drove away. When he was gone, I said, "Miz Hattie, y'all travelin' today?"

"We going to see my mama!" answered Grace-Anne, right happy about the thing.

Miz Hattie nodded. "That's a fact." Then she frowned and looked up the road. "I do hope that bus is on time."

"Why y'all takin' the bus, Miz Hattie?" I asked. "Y'all got a car and y'all could drive on down."

"Well, child, when Mr. McElroy was alive, we used to drive down all the time, but since he passed I just rather take the bus. I can't drive that car myself—my nerves are too bad—and Uncle Moses can't half see." She laughed. "As far as I would trust him to drive is from the house to this store and back. Believe me, it's a lot safer for us to take the bus." Then, leaving me with a sunshine smile, she took hold of Grace-Anne's hand and gone into the store.

Soon as they entered, Mr. John Wallace stopped his leaning against the counter and straightened up real gentlemanlike to greet her. She greeted him back, then they exchanged a few words about Miz Hattie traveling and about how both their families were doing. Then Mr. John Wallace said, "Anything in particular I can help you with today, Miz Hattie?"

"Well, I stopped in to get some candy for Grace-Anne here so she can have something while we're traveling."

"Yes, ma'am, we take care of that right now," said Mr. John Wallace. "Pretty little girl like Miss Grace-Anne deserve some sweets." He took a large glass jar of candy off the counter and bent down and held it in front of Grace-Anne so she could take whatever she pleased from the jar. Miz Hattie's eyes wandered to the counter and that summer-sky-blue hat Rudine had been admiring. Mr. John Wallace took note. "Anything else I can do for ya, Miz Hattie?"

"Well . . . I was just admiring this hat here . . ." She touched it real gentle-like. "It's so springtime . . ."

"Hat like that sure 'nough would put a little sunshine in this gloom," said Mr. Wallace. "Why don't you go 'head try it on, Miz Hattie? It sure would set well on your fine head of hair."

Miz Hattie turned plumb red. "Go on with you now, John Wallace! Can't much afford it anyway, not in these hard times."

"Well, it won't hurt nothin' t' try it on. There's a mirror right over here." He handed her the hat. "Go on, Miz Hattie, brighten up the place. It be a joy to see you in it."

Miz Hattie took the hat and placed it on that mop of red hair of hers. She pinned it down with a huge stickpin. Rudine and her mama were still in the store. I seen them watching.

"Now ain't that fine?" said Mr. Wallace. "Makes you look like a schoolgirl."

"Well, it sure is pretty all right," confessed Miz Hattie, primping at herself in the mirror. "It surely is. . . ."

While Miz Hattie was making up her mind about whether or not she was going to buy that hat, I seen Josias Williams coming up the road carrying a small bundle in his hand and all dressed up in his Sunday-go-to-meeting clothes. Josias was a full-grown man, some ten or more years over, but he wasn't yet married. He said he just ain't found his woman yet. Said, too, that was just as well 'cause there were so many mouths already to feed in his family, and that was sure enough the truth. There was a bunch of them living on a fourteen-acre spot of sharecropping land near to our place. 'Cause they were so close, Josias and me, sometimes we gone fishing down on the water Rosa Lee together. Josias and me, we was friends.

" 'Ey, Josias!" I called.

He seen me and he smiled that wide-toothed grin of his. "Wet 'nough for ya?" he asked, stepping onto the porch.

I asserted it was and he laughed. "Keep it up 'round here and we gonna hafta start building ourselves an ark, just like ole Noah!"

I smiled up at him, then took note of his bundle and asked straight out, "You travelin' today, Josias?"

"Yes, suh! Got me a chance to get myself a job. Gonna go lumberin' 'long on the Trace. Man say I be there today, I'm gonna have me a job!"

"Well, I sho' do hope you make it, Josias."

"Oh, I'm gonna make it all right. Spite all this here rain, Lord smilin' on me today! I knows He is!" Then he laughed and gone on in the store.

I got up and I gone in after him.

"Well, there, Josias," greeted Mr. John Wallace, "what got you all dressed up on a rainy weekday like this?"

"Well, suh, Mister John, I'm gonna take myself a trip!"

"That a fact?"

"Yes, suh!"

"Now where you get money to go takin' a trip, boy?"

"Scraped together ever' penny I could lay my hands on. Had to borrow a little bit, but it's gonna be worth it, 'cause I got a job waitin' on me!"

Pa began thumping the table with his fingers. Most times he done that when things ain't set too right with him. "Now, Josias," he said, "what kinda job you figure waitin' on you?"

Josias turned to Pa. "Well, Mr. Charlie, got a letter from my cousin doin' some lumberin' down long the Natchez Trace. He said I come on down, man'd hire me on and pay me cash money, so I'm sure 'nough goin'!"

Pa frowned. A lot of men were going begging for jobs these days. *White men.* And here Josias was talking about taking on a lumbering job along the Natchez Trace.

"What 'bout your plantin', boy?" asked Mr. John Wallace. "Ain't you got land to crop?"

"Ah, Mr. John, you know they's plenty of hands at home for that. They ain't gonna miss me none. Be better I'm off workin' makin' some cash money."

Pa thumped the table again. "What you doin' talkin' 'bout cash money, nigger? White men ain't hardly gettin' no cash money these days. What? You think you better'n a white man?"

The smile that had been shining all cross Josias's face sure gone quick. His eyes got big and I know'd he was scared. I had done seen that look before. "Why . . . why, no suh, Mr. Charlie. Ain't . . . ain't never thought such a thing."

"Then what you doin' standin' up there bald-faced lyin' for, sayin' you done got yourself a job?"

"Why, no suh, I . . . I ain't lyin'—"

"Then you sayin' you can get a job when a white man can't?"

Poor Josias, he ain't know'd what to say. I'd've been him, I'd've been in the same fix. Pa was a mean one when it come to colored folks. Josias glanced around at Rudine and her mama. They stepped back, looking scared. Miz Hattie turned from her mirror to look at him. Grace-Anne sucked on her candy stick and stared too.

Then Pa let that hand go. He slammed it hard against the table. "That what ya sayin'?"

"No! No—no, suh, Mr. Charlie! I—I ain't sayin' no such a thing! I ain't got me no job! I was jus' sayin' that, poppin' off my mouth, tryin' t' be big! I ain't got me no lumberin' job, Mr. Charlie, and I ain't got me no cash job whatsoever!"

"Then what you doin' takin' the bus for?"

Josias hung his head. "My cousin . . . my cousin he needin' help on his place. He been sickly all the winter and . . . and now he needin' me t' help get his crop planted."

Pa sneered, just like he know'd that all the time. R.W. and Melvin, they gone to grinning at Josias's humiliation and started mumbling about how Negroes lie. They was proud of Pa for making Josias admit the truth and they let him know it too. The other men, they done the same.

Josias, he got what he come in for and gone out again. I waited a few minutes, then I gone out too. I ain't liked the way Pa done talked to Josias. Josias was a nice man. He wasn't hurting nobody. But I know'd that was the way for Pa and the other men to talk that way to Josias and for Josias to take it. Colored folks seemed always to have to take that kind of talk. One time I seen Pa and Melvin and R.W. and a whole bunch drag a colored man down the road, beat him till he ain't hardly had no face on him 'cause he done stood up for himself and talked back. That ain't never set right with me, the way Pa done. It wasn't right and I just know'd that, but I ain't never let Pa know how I was feeling, 'cause Pa he could get awful riled and riled quick. Last thing a body wanted to do, blood or not, was to get on Pa's wrong side. You got on Pa's wrong side and you done had it.

I stepped out onto the porch and I seen Josias down at the far end leaning against a post. That bundle of his was set next to his feet. He seen me and put up his coat collar to warm his neck, then he crossed his arms and stared out at the crossroads, waiting on the bus. His mouth was clenched tight. He was looking right different from when he was inside the store. Then he had been scared. Now he was angry. I could see it all over him. I walked down and leaned on the post right side of him. "Josias," I said real quiet-like. "You got yourself that lumberin' job, ain'tcha?"

Josias flicked his eyes my way, but he ain't said nothing.

"You got that job all right. Wish . . . wish you ain't had to go lyin' on yourself, Josias."

Now Josias he looked on me long and hard. "You want me to say different? You want me dead?"

"Wh-what?"

" 'Cause I backlip yo' daddy, make him think I got somethin' he ain't got, that's what gonna happen to me, boy. Sho is. Here he a white man and me black as night. Happen t' me sure."

"But you got yo'self a right t' make some cash money!" I declared. "Shuckies! Ever'body wanna make some cash money, and you got a right much as anybody, Josias!"

Josias just stared at me, then looked back out at the road. He weren't speaking to me no more.

I moved away from him and gone on down to the other side of the steps and sat on the bench 'front of them store windows. For some while Josias just stood there leaning against his post, and I sat there on my bench and we ain't said nothing. It seemed mighty odd, the two of us on that porch and us not speaking. Rudine and her mama, they came out and gone down and stood near to Josias. After a while, Miz Hattie and Grace-Anne they came out too and they sat down beside me. Miz Hattie was wearing that springtime hat. "Jeremy!" called Grace-Anne. "You seen Granny's hat?"

I nodded.

"It sure pretty, ain't it?"

I glanced over at Rudine who was looking, then turned back to Miz Hattie. "Yeah . . . it sho is. . . ."

"Go on with you now!" laughed Miz Hattie, and I know'd she was feeling mighty fine-looking in that hat.

"It . . . it's the truth, Miz Hattie. You do look pretty," I said, and she thanked me for my praise.

I got up to leave the bench, but then Grace-Anne held out her small paper bag in front of me. "Here, Jeremy," she said, "here, have some of my lemon drops."

She was such a sweet thing of a little girl, but I ain't had my mind much on lemon drops. I reached into the bag anyways, took a couple of pieces of candy, thanked her kindly, then walked on 'cross the porch to the edge and leaned against a post, just like Josias was doing. I know'd I couldn't fault Miz Hattie 'cause Rudine couldn't try on that hat, but I felt bad about it just the same, just like I felt bad about Josias. I wanted to go talk some more to Josias before he got on that bus and left, but he weren't having nothing to do with me, so I just stood there leaned against my post, watching him and Rudine.

After a while I seen more folks coming up the road. It was that boy, Stacey Logan, with his grandmama and his sister, Cassie, and them brothers of his, Christopher-John and Little Man. Stacey, he was ten, same age as me. Cassie, she was 'bout seven and Christopher-John, maybe five, and Little Man no more than four. Their family owned a whole bunch of acres just west of us and that was something, them being colored. Folks said they'd been owning that land for near to fifty years, but them having land, when we was tenants ourselves living on somebody else's place, ain't never set too well with Pa. Being tenants wasn't bad as being sharecroppers seeing that we owned our own mule, paid for our own seed and such, and paid our rent for the land in cash money 'stead of crops; still, we ain't owned the land we farmed like the Logans done. Pa, he said it wasn't right for Negroes to have more than white folks, said that 'cause of that land them Logans had got the big head and walked around prideful all the time, thinking they was good as white folks. 'Cause of that, Pa, he ain't never took a liking to them. Me, though, I did. They was a fascination to me. They had a way 'bout them.

On this day they was looking like they was traveling too. Their grandmama was carrying a satchel in one hand and an umbrella held over herself with the other. Stacey, he was lugging a burlap sack and the rest of them younguns was each carrying a tin can and all four of 'em wore hooded calfskins to keep water shed of 'em. I perked up some seeing them coming. They stepped up to the porch, and I give a nod. Their grandmama—Caroline her name was—she give a nod back, lowered her umbrella, and gone on down to the other end of the porch to stand with Josias and Rudine and her mama. Stacey, he spoke, but them other younguns ain't said a word, like one body of them speaking was

enough. They just looked at me and hurried on down the porch after their grandmama. Stacey was 'bout to follow, but then I got up my voice and I said, " 'Ey . . . 'ey, Stacey, y'all travelin' today?"

He give me a look like it wasn't none of my business, but he done answered me anyway. "Big Ma, she is."

"Where she headin'?" I asked. It wasn't that I was curious to know. I was just up there holding conversation. Stacey, he give me another look.

"Big Ma's sister, she low sick. Big Ma goin' down t' tend to her."

"Well, I . . . I sho hopes she be all right . . . get well right quick. . . ."

"Thank ya," he said, then he moved away. "I gotta go."

I give him a nod and he gone down to the other end of the porch to join the rest of his folks. Wasn't long after that the bus coming down from Jackson showed up. The bus driver got out and gone into the store and when he come back, he spoke right polite to Miz Hattie and Grace-Anne and said they could get on the bus.

"Jeremy, help us with these bags, will you, child?" asked Miz Hattie.

"Yes'm, sure thing!" I answered quick, happy to do it. I took up a piece of their baggage and the bus driver, he picked up the other and we all got on the bus. The bus was near to full, but Miz Hattie found two seats right near the front. The bus driver, he seen Miz Hattie and Grace-Anne settled down, then he took their money for the ride, wished them a fine trip and stepped out again. I stayed on a minute to talk to Miz Hattie and Grace-Anne, but I could hear the bus driver outside as he took the colored folks' money and told them they could get on now. Once those folks had done paid their money, the bus driver stepped back to the porch and stood there talking to Mr. John Wallace. Josias, Rudine, and her mama got on and gone straight to the back. Stacey's and them's grandmama got on last and all the younguns was with her, helping her with her satchel and that burlap bag Stacey carried. Their grandmama gone on past me. So did Christopher-John and Little Man. But then as that Cassie come up, she stopped, and she said: "Wait up there a minute, Big Ma! Here's a seat. Here's a seat right here!"

Everybody on the bus turned eyes on them. Their grand-mama Caroline looked around, seen them eyes, and she let

loose on Cassie. "Hush up, girl!" she snapped. "Ya hush up and come on!" Then she turned and kept on to the back of the bus where all the other colored folks was seated.

But Cassie she ain't let up. She ain't moved. "But what ya wanna sit all the way back there for, Big Ma?" she cried. "Can't see nothin' from *waaay* back there. This here seat much better'n . . ."

Stacey, he come behind her and he give her a good poke, then he grabbed her hand and jerked her on. She yanked back, fussing furious. "Boy, what's the matter with you?" she screamed. "You got no cause to be hittin' on me . . ."

"Girl, hush!" Stacey hissed at her. "Them's *white* folks' seats!"

He said that to her and his eyes fell flat on mine, and I could see he was powerful angry, just like Josias. Cassie, she looked back at that seat she had been wanting for her grandmama, then she looked at me too, and followed Stacey on down the aisle to the back of the bus. I turned back to Miz Hattie, who done shook her head and sighed. She made Grace-Anne turn around and stop staring, then she said her good-byes to me and wished me well. "You be good now," she said.

"Yes'm," I assured her, and I gone to the door.

" 'Bye, Jeremy!" hollered Grace-Anne, waving that little hand at me.

I looked at her with them shining little curls and I give a wave back and smiled. " 'Bye," I said. "S-see y'all when ya get back." Then I got off.

Stacey, Cassie, Christopher-John, and Little Man come right after. They had set them cans they had been carrying on the porch while they helped their grandmama on the bus. Now they gone back to the porch to gather them up; then they just stood there waiting and staring up at the bus. Their grandmama opened up a back window and poked her head out. "What y'all doin'?" she said.

Cassie spoke right up. "Waitin' for y'all to leave, Big Ma!"

That ain't set well with their grandmama Caroline. "Stacey, you take these here younguns on!" she ordered. "Y'all don't need t' be waitin' here till I go. Now y'all go on, so's ya can get back home and help ya mama. Miz Georgia, she waitin' on that milk now!"

"But, Big Ma," protested Little Man, "we wants to see y'all off!"

"Yes, ma'am," attested Christopher-John. "We just wait right here till the bus leave—"

"I tole y'all not to wait! No tellin' how long this bus be sittin' here. 'Sides, ya know I don't want y'all standin' up here front of this store. Now do like I say! I see y'all in a few days."

They ain't moved.

She got to threatening. "I gotta get off this bus t' make y'all mind? Stacey, boy, you do like I say and get these younguns 'way from here!"

Now they stirred, sure enough. "We loves ya, Big Ma!" they hollered up to her.

"Well, I loves y'all too. Now y'all run on 'long now. I wants y'all gone from here 'fore I am. Don't y'all worry. I be all right."

"Yes, ma'am," they said real soft-like as they slowly moved away.

"And y'all go straight t' home after y'all leave Miz Georgia's! Y'all hear me now?"

"Yes, ma'am, Big Ma, we hear!" they answered. Then, looking kind of sorrowful, they backed on away, waving their good-byes, turned, and moved slowly on past the store and down the road toward the bridge. Once they stopped and looked back to see if that ole bus done moved, but it ain't and they gone on.

Me, I gone back to my post, leaned against it hard, and stared down the bridge road. The fog was coming up thick now and I could hardly see Stacey and them as they headed for the bridge. I couldn't make out the bridge at all. On a sudden, I had a longing to go try and talk to them Logans, and I left that post to stand by itself and shot down the road after them. As I ran, I seen two wagons coming out of the fog. It was the Henry Amoses, folks I know'd from over by Smellings Creek. One of their boys, ole green-eyed Shorty Amos, was in class with me over at Jefferson Davis. I give a wave and a shout to Shorty and his folks, and they give a wave and a shout back and they rolled on. I wondered if they was traveling today too, seemed like so many folks was. They gone on, then I hollered at Stacey and them. " 'Ey, y'all wait up!" The four of them stopped sure enough, but they ain't looked none too happy to see me. "Where y'all headed?" I asked, catching up, even though I already had that figured.

Stacey, he done give me that look, like I was asking too many questions again. "We got t' 'tend business for Big Ma."

But that Cassie, she spoke right up; she wasn't so closed mouthed as Stacey. "We goin' over to Miz Georgia's. We takin' her some milk." Then she gone on strutting toward the bridge; she done had her say. That girl, she had plenty of mouth on her and she never paid me much attention one way or the other, 'ceptin' to speak her mind.

"Yeah," said Christopher-John, smiling right friendly at me. He was a chubby kind of a little fella and a right pleasant sort. "They cow ain't got no more milk and they got a whole buncha younguns over there to Miz Georgia's, and Big Ma, she say younguns need plenty of milk to grow right."

"And we got *plenty* of milk!" declared Little Man. Never minding his four years, he was a boy on the prideful side and Stacey know'd it too. He give me a look, then give one to Little Man, letting him know wasn't no need to go bragging. Little Man, he understood that look and he ain't said another word, but I could see in his eyes he wasn't regretting a word of his bragging. That was the way he was.

I kind of smiled, liking his prideful ways, then I took up conversation as I walked along with them. "It sure is rainin', ain't it?"

Stacey, he give me a quick look, like he was wondering what I was walking along with them for, then agreed. "That's a fact," he said.

"Can't hardly see the bridge for all this here fog," I commented.

"Don't need to see it," declared that Cassie. "Anything look poor as that bridge don't need to get seen."

Christopher-John, he slowed his steps. "I'm scairt of it."

"I ain't," said Little Man.

"That's 'cause you ain't got the good sense 'nough yet to be scared," decided Cassie. "Shoot! You give that old bridge one good sneeze, it likely to fall down."

She was right. It was a rickety old thing, that wooden bridge, and it was good that it was only wide enough for one vehicle to cross it at a time. Story was it had been built way before the War 'tween the States, and it looked like it ain't had much work done on it since. As we neared the bridge, the rain beat down harder and the fog settled all around, and we could hardly see a thing. Limbs of the trees, all weighted down with water, hung low, making going slow. We reached the bridge and stopped, not setting foot on it as we stared across the waters of the Rosa Lee. The creek was on the rise. Stacey, he took the first step onto the bridge. "Y'all come on," he said. "Might's well get on 'cross."

Right then, Christopher-John, he gone to whining. "I don't wanna go on that bridge!"

"Gotta go on it," Stacey told him. "Gotta cross it to get to Miz Georgia's."

"Well, then, I—I'll jus' wait right here for y'all," Christopher-John said.

"Naw, you won't neither!" exclaimed Stacey. "Now come on! Give me your hand." Stacey, he done put his foot down now and wasn't nothing poor little ole Christopher-John could've done to dispute that. So, reluctant-like, he took Stacey's hand, and all them Logans stepped onto the bridge.

I gone with them. We took some slow steps, listening all the while to the creaking of the wooden planks beneath our feet; then that Cassie started up grumbling. "Now what if a car or a truck or somethin' come 'long while we on this thing? Can't see the other side."

"We hear whatever comin'," Stacey told her.

"With all this rain?" she asked.

"Folks drivin' in a fog this way, Cassie, always honk their horns."

Christopher-John, he looked up all big-eyed. "You— you sure, Stacey?"

"Yeah . . . got nothin' to worry 'bout."

"Nothin' to worry 'bout if the horn's workin'," Cassie took note.

Stacey, he done give her a look like she was a pure bother to him, but she ain't seemed to care.

"And what 'bout if a wagon come?" she gone on. "Wagon ain't got no horn."

Look like to me, Stacey he was getting right put out with her. "Cassie, wagon ain't got no horn cause it don't need no horn! It don't go fast like a car! Now come on

39

and just hush up! We gotta get this milk up to Miz Georgia's and get on home!"

Then Little Man he give a shout, set down his bucket and dashed right up to the rail. Little Man wasn't much afraid of nothing. He picked up a rock and threw it off the bridge, then leaned against the rail and stared down into the water trying to see where that rock done gone.

"Man!" Stacey let go of Christopher-John's hand and ran over to the rail to rescue Little Man. "Get 'way from there!"

Obedient-like, Little Man stepped back, pointing at the water. "Ya see, Stacey? Ya see how far I done throw'd that rock?" He was sure enough proud of himself.

Cassie, she run over to the rail and looked over too. "Owwww, y'all oughta see this water!"

"I don't wanna see it!" Christopher-John yelled back. "I don't even wanna see nothin' on this bridge!" he declared, and saying that, he took off back toward the store.

Stacey, he gone after him. Cassie, she ain't paid no attention to neither one. She had her eyes set straight down, looking at the bridge. I gone over to see what she was studying on so hard and I seen where one of the planks had rotted through, leaving a fine view of the water flowing beneath the bridge. Cassie, I had learned a long while ago, was a mighty curious girl, so I wasn't hardly surprised when she leaned down to get a better look, then lay right flat down on the bridge and peered through that hole.

"Y'all come see!" she hollered.

I know'd she was talking to her brothers, not me, but I got down flat on the bridge too, next to her, and give a look anyways. The water looked right close, like it was 'bout to leap up and snatch us. Little Man come dashing over as well, but before he got to us and the hole, Stacey, tugging Christopher-John after him by the hand, caught Little Man and yelled: "Cassie! Get up from there, off'n that bridge!"

Cassie, she looked around. "Ah, come on, Stacey, take a look. Water ain't never been this high before."

But Stacey, he put his foot down hard now. He had hold of both Little Man and Christopher-John, and he wasn't about to be putting up with Cassie. "Cassie, I said

get up from there!" he hollered. "Now I want y'all to stop foolin' round! Christopher-John, open your eyes! Little Man, quit your wiggling! Cassie, come on! We gotta get this milk to Miz Georgia's and get home. Now, let's go!"

'Minded now of their mission, Cassie, Christopher-John, and Little Man done as Stacey ordered. Cassie, she got herself up, Christopher-John opened his eyes, and Little Man fell right into line and the four of them continued on across the bridge. They ain't paid me no more attention and I ain't gone after. Still, I give them another holler and they looked back. "Y'all take care now!" I called.

"Yeah . . . you too!" Stacey answered, like he'd forgotten I was even along. Then they gone on, walking into the fog. I ain't tried to follow. I know'd I wasn't welcomed. All I wanted was to be friends with them Logans, let 'em know how I was feeling 'bout 'em, but I just couldn't seem to get no way close to 'em. I watched them till I couldn't see them no more; then I turned and headed back to the Wallace store.

By the time I got to the store, I found there was a bit of a ruckus going on. The bus was still there, and the bus driver was hollering to high heaven. "Now I ain't gonna tell y'all again," he cried. "Y'all gonna get off! Ain't room for everybody!"

I eased on up, wondering what was happening. Then I seen the bus was full up and I seen too Mr. and Miz Henry Amos and a bunch of their red-haired children standing on the porch loaded down with traveling gear. They looked to be waiting to get on. The bus driver stood inside the bus, right up front by his seat. Standing there in the aisle was more of that Amos clan.

"Come on!" the bus driver ordered.

I thought he was maybe talking to the Amoses standing in the aisle, but they ain't moved. Folks sitting in back, the colored folks, they moved and they moved quick. They give up their seats and come forward. The Amoses moved on back and sat down. The colored folks, they got off the bus. Stacey's and them's grandmama, she got off too. She got off without a word, carrying her satchel in one hand and that burlap bag in the other. She looked out, up and down the road. She looked at me, but she ain't said nothing. Her face was set, and it was set hard. She turned and moved slowly on down the road, away from the store, away from the bus toward home. Her head was straight up and she ain't looked back, not one time. Rudine and her mama, they got off too. So did all the other colored folks traveling down from Jackson. I waited for Josias to step on down, but he ain't come. I give a hard look inside and I seen him still sitting on that backseat and that bus driver, he done seen him too.

"Nigger!" he hollered at Josias. "Ain't I done tole you to get off this bus?"

"Y-yes, suh. But I—I done paid my money . . ."

"You get it back."

"Y-yes, suh, but I . . . I gots to go on *this* bus! I gots to go today!"

"What for?"

"I . . . I got business," acclaimed Josias. "I got awful 'portant business."

The driver, he laughed. "Onliest important business I done ever know'd a nigger to have is with a jug of liquor or some gal. Which one waitin' on you, boy?"

Josias ain't answered. He just done sat there on that backseat, his head hung all low. I know'd how come he wanted to go so bad, but I know'd too, he couldn't tell that bus driver how come. Wouldn't have made no difference anyways, I reckon.

" 'Ey, boy, you hear me talkin' t' ya?" Josias, he reared up his head. "What business ya got?"

Josias stood. He picked up his bundle of clothes and he give up his seat. He took himself some slow steps to the front of the bus. I moved over to the door waiting to say my spell to him, but he still ain't got off. He stopped hisself right front of that driver and he gone to pleading. "Please, boss . . . I got to get to the Trace t'day. Please, boss. I done got my ticket. I done made all my plans. Folks spectin' me. I gots t' go on this bus!"

"Nigger, I said you gettin' off."

"Boss, please . . ."

That bus driver, he ain't give Josias chance to say no more. He jerked Josias forward to the door, put his foot flat to Josias's backside, and give him a push like Josias wasn't no more 'n a piece of baggage, and Josias, he gone sprawling down them steps into the mud. The bus driver, he throw'd Josias's bundle after him, his ticket money too.

I ain't know'd what to say. Josias, he done looked at me, then he picked hisself up. He picked up his bundle and his money and walked away, back toward the bridge. "Josias!" I called. "Wait on up a minute, will ya? Josias!"

I run after him but Josias, he ain't stopped.

"Josias! I'm right sorry! Sorry 'bout you can't go on that bus! Josias, ya hear me . . . ?"

He stopped now and looked back at me. I stopped too. "Well, that's jus' the way, ain't it?" he done said.

I nodded that it was and he gone on, and I just stood there staring after him. I was staring so hard on him I ain't heard Pa coming. Next thing I know'd, Pa was all over me. Pa could hit ya' blind from any side and he done got me good this time.

"Pa!" I yelped.

"Ain't I done told you 'bout snivelin' after niggers?"

"But, Pa, I wasn't—"

He struck me again. "Don't you backlip me!" He boxed my ears good.

"No, suh, Pa."

"Now you leave off being so friendly with these niggers, ya hear me? They got they place in this world and we got our'n and they place ain't 'long 'side us 'cause they ain't the same as us. You understand me, boy?"

I hung my head and took to studying my feet. "Y-yes, suh, Pa." But that wasn't the truth. I ain't understood. No, suh, I sure ain't. I liked that boy Stacey and that girl Cassie and little ole Christopher-John and Little Man. I liked Josias too. But I ain't told Pa that. To me, folks was just folks, but Pa he jus' ain't stood for no wrong way of thinking, so I ain't spoke up.

Pa gone on back into the store, and I looked up from studying my feet. I looked back at the store, then up toward the bridge. The fog was so thick I couldn't see the bridge or Josias, but I run for them anyway. Soon's I figured I was out of Pa's hearing, I started to calling Josias. I know'd he was there up ahead and I know'd he heard me, but he ain't waited for me and he ain't answered. I ain't give up though. I kept on running.

Then I heard the bus. I looked back, done seen its lights coming, and I jumped out the way onto the bank at the side of the road. That ole bus it passed and I jumped right on back down again and gone speeding after it. The bus headed on to the bridge. I done too. I ran, ready to bust

my whole heart out trying to catch up with Josias. I run like a lightnin' strike.

I got to the bridge, and I got to tiring. My ole feet just couldn't seem to pick theyselves up and flatten down one more time. I couldn't see Josias, but I could see that bus shooting 'cross the bridge like it was scairt something was 'bout to catch up with it. I put all my mind to moving my feet, to racing that bus, but the bus it broke clean away from me. It gone too fast, I reckon, 'cause it wasn't half across when it spun out crazy, zigging and zagging on them rotten planks, then zinged off like a bullet into the railing, smashed through it, and shot straight down into the waters of the Rosa Lee.

I ran toward the broken railing. Josias, he come through the fog, back from the other way. Josias, he done caught me as I run up 'cause I was flying now and he hadn't've caught me, I'd've gone over into that water too. Josias held me and we stood there staring off that broken rail with the rain pounding down on us. The bus was all bellied up like a dead catfish and was sinking fas
I thought of Miz Hattie and Grace-Anne, and I s
"Josias! All them folks! Josias! They gonna die

Josias, he put his hands on my shoulders and calmed me down, made me remember I was a man. "Now, Jeremy, you go on back t' that store," he said. "You go right now, ya hear? Get your pa, your brothers, ever'body else ya can! Tell 'em the bus done gone off the bridge!"

"But Miz Hattie and Grace-Anne, Josias—"

"I see to 'em. I'm gon' go right on down t' see 'bout 'em all. Now you run, boy! You run fast now!"

I wasn't hardly in my right mind when I nodded that I would, but somehow my legs done straightened out and Josias done pushed me away from him, and I gone sprinting back across that bridge and over that slop of a road. I weren't tired no more, but I was plenty scairt. 'Fore I run all the way down to the store, I looked back to the bridge. There was a break in the fog, but I couldn't see Josias. He had already slipped into the water. I run on and gone to hollering, "Pa! The bus done gone off the bridge! Pa! Pa! Come quick, Pa! The bus done gone off the bridge!"

What with all the rain beating down, ain't nobody heard me till I got on the porch and stormed inside, and Pa, he ain't looked too pleased with me. He squinted his eyes and barked: "Boy, what kinda ruckus you carryin' on?"

Another time, I'd've gone to stammering, but wasn't no time for stammering now. "Pa, come quick!" I shouted loud and I shouted hard. "The bus, it done gone off the bridge! I seen it, Pa! Jus' now! I seen it!"

"Oh, Lord!" exclaimed Mr. John Wallace. "Ya sure? Ya ain't funnin' now, boy, is ya?"

"I seen it, Mr. John!" I screamed back. "Me and Josias, we both done seen it!"

The men ain't waited no longer. They all jumped up and run outside for the bridge. I was near to out of breath, but I ain't took me no time to rest. I shot down that road right with them and I ain't slowed down. We come to the bridge, and Pa and Mr. Wallace, R.W. and Melvin and the other grown-up folks, they run straight for where the bus gone off. The railing, course it was gone and all there was left was a big open space. The men, they gone for that hole and stopped just short of going off theyselves into the water. They all stood there like they ain't 'spected to see that bus, but it was right there. I ain't lied. Then Pa, he took charge. "Melvin, R.W.! Y'all go the west bank! Rest of us, we take the east!"

My brothers and all the other men, they done obeyed his words quick! And quick as spit, they gone to running. But 'fore Pa gone into the waters, he looked back at me. "Jeremy, boy!" he yelled. "You go on up t' the church there and ring that bell! Ring it loud, ya hear me? Ring it so's everybody round'll hear! Ring it so's folks'll come!"

"Yes, suh, Pa!" I promised, and he gone into the water.

I started to do like Pa said, but then I seen Stacey and them come running onto the bridge, back from delivering their milk. They ran right to that busted rail, and they was hollering, "What happened? What done happened?" Then they seen the bus and they screamed. *"Big Maaaa!"*

I run right over. "She all right!" I cried. "Your grand-mama, she fine! She gone on home!"

They looked like they ain't believed me.

"But . . . but she was on that bus," said Stacey.

I shook my head. "Naw . . . naw, Stacey, she wasn't."

"She was so too on that bus!" Cassie, she screamed back.

"Naw . . ." I looked at them feeling right ashamed to tell them what happened, but I done it. "Wasn't . . . wasn't 'nough room for everybody, and the bus driver, he . . . he done made all the colored folks get off. Your grandmama, Josias, Rudine, and her mama, they all got off."

The four of them just stood there staring at me, as if they couldn't trust my words.

"What? Y'all don't believe me?" I said. "I wouldn't lie to y'all! 'Specially not 'bout somethin' like this! Josias, he down there, ask him y'all don't believe me! Ask Josias! He was headin' back to home when that bus gone over and he down there now pullin' folks out! Y'all don't believe me, just y'all ask him!"

Stacey looked over the bridge. The fog had drifted back and there was no sign of Josias. He looked at me again, then he said, real quiet-like, "Come on. We goin' home."

"But, Stacey, Big Ma—" started Cassie.

Stacey's eyes were set right on me. "She at home," he said, and I know'd he believed me. Then, without another word, he took off streaking down the bridge and Cassie, Christopher-John, and Little Man, they was right behind him, running hard as they could for home. I started to follow after 'cause the church was back up that way, but then the fog shifted and I seen Josias come out of the water and he was carrying a small bundle that looked like it wasn't no more than a wet doll with sunshine hair,

and I ain't moved. He laid his bundle down on the bank, real gentle-like. He laid it right down next to a still, white body with a summer-sky-blue hat pinned to its hair. He laid it right next side to Miz Hattie.

"Josias!" I screamed, and he looked up to the bridge and me standing there. Then I run down from the bridge, shrieking to the heaven above. "Miz Hattie! Miz Hattie! Grace-Anne!" I run right for them bodies lying so still and unmoving on the bank. Josias, though, he caught up with me before I got to them.

"Hold on there, boy," he said. "Hold on."

"Josias, they ain't . . . they ain't—"

"Yes, suh, boy . . . they is."

I shook my head and looked up at him. "But how come, Josias? *How come?*"

Josias, he shook his head too and he give a mighty sigh. "Ain't for me t' know. Can't go questionin' the ways of the Lord. Onliest thing I know is that the good book, it say the Lord He work in mighty mysterious ways."

"But, Josias—"

"Jeremy!"

I looked to the other side of the water. It was Pa.

"Ain't you gone yet?" he hollered. "I said go ring that bell! Now, get!"

I looked up at Josias. He patted my shoulder and said real soft-like, "Go on, boy. Go on and ring the bell."

I glanced again at Miz Hattie and Grace-Anne, again at Josias, and I turned and I ran back up the bank to the road. I ran down past the store, ran down toward the school of Jefferson Davis and the church. The rain was beating hard on me now and I was glad of it, 'cause I was crying hard too. Weren't much difference between rain and tears, and I ain't needed to wipe neither one away. I run straight up to the church, straight up to the belfry and I rung that bell, rung that bell as hard as I could, and all the while I was crying 'cause I couldn't understand nothing about the day, about how come Miz Hattie and Grace-Anne was on that bus, and Josias, and Stacey's and them's grandmama and Rudine and her mama wasn't. Mysterious ways, Josias done said. Well, if the Lord was punishing, how come Grace-Anne and Miz Hattie? They ain't hurt nobody.

I rung that bell till I figured I couldn't ring it no more, then as folks started coming in answer to the bell, I run with them back to the Rosa Lee. Josias was still there, hauling folks out. I gone down to the bank, took one more look at Miz Hattie and Grace-Anne, then I gone to join Josias. I slipped into the water and give him a hand.

Me and Josias, we was there all the day.

Mildred D. Taylor

has written three previous novels about the Logans: the Newbery Medal-winning *Roll of Thunder, Hear My Cry*, the Coretta Scott King Award-winning *Let the Circle Be Unbroken*, and the just-published *The Road to Memphis*. Cassie Logan is also featured in two short books, *Song of the Trees*, a *New York Times* Outstanding Book of the Year, and *The Friendship*, winner of the *Boston Globe/Horn Book* Award. Ms. Taylor received the Christopher Award for *The Gold Cadillac*. In 1988 she was honored by the Children's Book Council "for a body of work that has examined significant social issues and presented them in outstanding books for young readers."

Mildred D. Taylor was born in Jackson, Mississippi, and grew up in Toledo, Ohio. After two years in Ethiopia with the Peace Corps, Ms. Taylor entered the University of Colorado's School of Journalism, from which she received her Master of Arts degree. She now lives in Colorado.

Max Ginsburg

has received a number of awards including the Gold Medal from the Society of Illustrators in New York. He has exhibited his paintings in one-man shows and also has created magazine illustrations and book covers, including the jacket as well as the interior art for Ms. Taylor's *The Friendship*. In addition to painting, Mr. Ginsburg also teaches art in New York City, where he now lives.

With love and gratitude

To

From

Mother

new seasons™

Picture credits:

Book jacket illustrated by Robin Moro.

Art Resource: Fine Art Photographic Library, London; Giraudon; Erich Lessing; **Aaron Boyd; Bridgeman Art Library, London/New York:** *The Eleventh Hour, the Eleventh Day of the Eleventh Month* by W. Percy Day, Harris Museum and Art Gallery, Preston, Lancashire, UK; *Falling Apple Blossoms* by Hamilton, Private Collection, Phillips, Fine Art Auctioneers, New York; *Sunrise, Brent at Low Water* by Julian Novorol, Private Collection; *Lunch al fresco* by © Ann Patrick, Collection of Andrew McIntosh Patrick, UK; *Beach Scene, II* by Dorothea Sharp, Private Collection; *New Baby (2),* by Carol Walklin, Private Collection; **Vivian Browning; Corbis:** Archivo Iconografico, S.A.; The Barnes Foundation, Pennsylvania; Alexander Burkatowski; Geoffrey Clements; Francis G. Mayer; Collection of Andrew McIntosh Patrick; Philadelphia Museum of Art; Dick Reed; Kirsten Soderlind; **Drew-Brook-Cormack Associates; Michael Jaroszko; Roger-Viollet/Getty Images; SuperStock:** Cummer Museum of Art & Gardens; David David Gallery; Elizabeth Barakah Hodges; Huntington Library; Henry John Peterson III

Contributing writers:

Elaine Creasman, June Eaton, Lain Chroust Ehmann, Jan Goldberg, Jennifer Ouellette, June Stevenson

When a new mother gazes into the eyes of her newborn and their fingertips gently meet, she understands for the first time the depth of her own mother's love for her.

$\mathcal{T}$he joyful job of being a
mother is a priceless challenge
that comes with her little gift
from heaven.

Moms belong to a special club.
No matter how old they are,
where they were born, or what
language they speak, they share
similar hopes and dreams for
their children.

Recipe for the Perfect Mother

one part Mother Teresa

one part Betty Crocker

one part Dear Abby

one part Arnold Schwarzenegger

Mix thoroughly, and bake under extreme pressure

until firm yet soft in the middle.

RECIPES

A mother knows that sometimes
the best thing to say is nothing at all and
the best thing to do is listen.

Her Photo

My mother: a vision of goodness wrapped in sunlight and smiles.

One of the biggest lessons
a mother teaches a child is
how to laugh. One of the
biggest lessons a child
teaches a mother is how to
laugh at herself.

Mothers help their children
take first steps across rooms—
and along the paths of life.

To a child, a mom has amazing powers:
She can make the scary monster
under the bed disappear the instant
she walks in the room.

Motherhood can be challenging, like keeping your balance on a
sailboat: Just when you think you know your footing, the winds shift
and you must adjust all over again.

A wise mother
knows when to
protect her children
from bad decisions
and when to let
them learn from
their own mistakes.

A mother is the heartbeat
of her home, the pulse of
her family's existence.

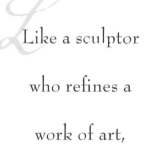

Like a sculptor

who refines a

work of art,

a mother works

to prepare her child

to make a positive

mark on the world.

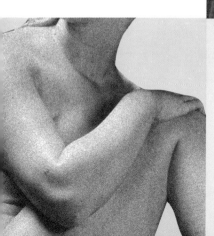

A mom is her
children's own
special angel,
guiding, guarding,
and protecting
each of them.

One who knows a mother's loving care
Knows that God is near.
One who knows a mother's lilting voice
Hears the angel's song.

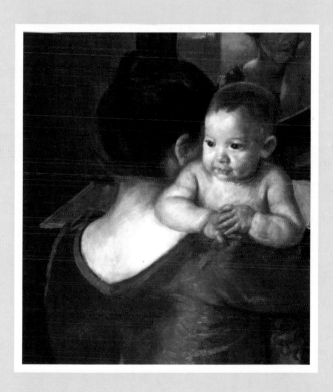

To a child, the sweetest
sound in the world is
Mother's voice saying,
"I love you."

Mothers are caretakers of the future. They nourish the seeds that will become tomorrow's garden and water them with an occasional tear. They pull the weeds of discontent and fertilize with plenty of love so their children will grow up healthy and happy.

Motherhood is the only occupation
where overtime is paid in
peanut-butter-and-jelly-coated hugs.

Few places on earth seem safer than
the arms of a loving mother.

A mother is she who can take the place of all others
but whose place no one else can take.

CARDINAL GASPARD MERMILLOD

Her Photo

The bond between mother and child is
indescribable, indestructible, and irreversible.

Moms have long-range radar.
They understand the link
between today's choices and
tomorrow's results.

I dream what I dream because of my mother.
I have what I have because of my mother.
I love how I love because of my mother.
I am who I am because of my mother.

The only thing stronger than a
mom's will is a child's smile.

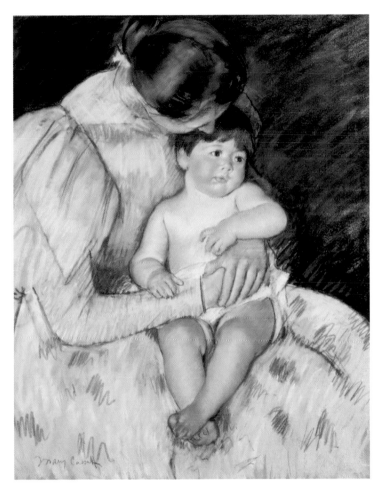

A mother possesses coolness in her palms to soothe fevered brows,
a comfortable lap to hold her children safe, and sturdy shoulders
to nestle tired little heads.

Mothers are like air traffic controllers— constantly adjusting their children's courses to ensure everyone lands on time and in one piece.

Never underestimate the value of a happy mother.

A bouquet of spring dandelions presented by her child's small grubby hand is like a dozen beautiful roses to a mother.

Like the lovely melody
of birds singing on a
sunny morning is the
sound of mother and
child laughing together.

Being a mom means being the counselor, mediator, chef, fashion coordinator, cleaner, receptionist, entertainer, and chauffeur...all before noon!

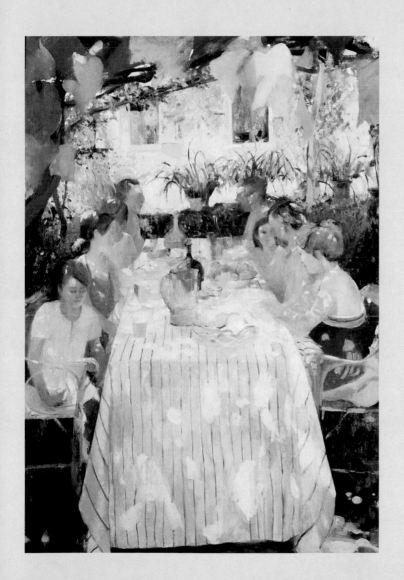

From broccoli to
brownies and
popcorn to pizza,
no matter what kind
of cook she is,
a mom makes
everything taste better.

Motherhood:
All love begins and ends there.

ROBERT BROWNING

Mothers who reflect
God's love see
themselves mirrored
in the eyes of their
children.

A mother would rather have her child's kisses on her cheek
than diamonds on her neck.

Her Photo

How do you thank the woman who dedicates her life to you,
makes sacrifices so you can have the best,
and still loves you immeasurably?
You call her "Mom."

The finest gift a
mother can give
her children is
the freedom to
be themselves.

As any self-respecting robin knows, a mother's most important job is to force her children out of the nest.

Follow in your mother's footsteps,
You will learn to walk tall.
Walk beside your mother proudly,
You will learn to run swiftly.
Run ahead of your mother's shadow,
You will learn to fly boldly.

*M*y mother had a
great deal of trouble
with me,
but I think she
enjoyed it.

MARK TWAIN

To a mom, each of her
children is a gift that
makes the world a
decidedly better place.

Moms always see the best in you,
No matter what you say or do.

A mother deserves
the Nobel Peace Prize.
She serves as
arbitrator, chief
negotiator, and
peacemaker in every
conflict between
her children.

Who ran to help me when I fell,
And would some pretty story tell,
Or kiss the place to make it well?
My Mother.

ANN TAYLOR, "MY MOTHER"

Unconditional love from Mom
is a precious gift to a child.

A good mother knows how to give
her child peace of mind rather than
"a piece of her mind."

In her garden of love, a mother grows as many blooms
as her children can pick.

The paradox of motherhood:
The more you love your
children, the more you must
be willing to let them go.

Enjoying a mother's love is like basking in
the radiance of the sun on a summer's day.

$\mathcal{M}$ "Mother"—the one who pulls the heart toward home.

Her Photo

A mother binds her
children to her with
cords of trust that
stretch like elastic and
protect like steel.

A mother's job is not to
solve all her children's
problems but to stand
by with her first-aid kit
full of love while they
try to solve them on
their own.

A mom's capacity for giving without expecting anything
in return is endless.

Skillful mothering often means learning that when you think you're at the end of your rope you should have faith, let go, and enjoy the ride!

As a child, you followed behind your mother
and copied every move.
As a teenager, you raced ahead of her
because you knew all the answers.
As an adult, you walk beside her
because she is your friend.

The mother's heart is the child's schoolroom.

HENRY WARD BEECHER